This book belongs to
my friend:

A NOTE TO PARENTS

Reading to your child every day is a simple yet effective way to ensure good lifelong reading habits. Identifying letters is one of the first steps a child takes towards learning words and eventually reading independently. In *Blue's Clues ABCs,* Blue and her friends play an alphabet game. Encourage your child to play along!

Each page of *Blue's Clues ABCs* highlights a different letter of the alphabet. Words starting with the featured letter are found in bold type. As you read the story, point out these words and the letter they start with to your child, and repeat the sound that each letter makes. Have your child find the matching pictures, and on the last page, identify the entire alphabet hidden in the picture.

Create an environment in your home that makes learning letters and words enjoyable. Play an eye-spy game using letters; for example, "I see something that starts with E." Buy some magnetic letters for your refrigerator, sing the *Alphabet Song,* and practice writing letters with chalk or crayons. Allow your child the space and time to explore words and books at her own pace. She will be reading on her own before you know it.

Learning Fundamental:  **reading + language**

For more parent and kid-friendly activities, go to www.nickjr.com.

Blue's Clues ABCs

Published by Scholastic Inc., 90 Old Sherman Turnpike, Danbury, CT 06816

ISBN 0-7172-6623-0

Printed in the U.S.A.

First Scholastic Printing, November 2002

Blue's Clues ABC's

by
Tish Rabe

illustrated by
Jennifer Oxley

SCHOLASTIC INC.
New York Toronto London Auckland Sydney
Mexico City New Delhi Hong Kong Buenos Aires

Blue and her friends are glad you came!
They're ready to play an alphabet game.
Will you play along and help them see
Things that start with each letter from *A* to *Z*?

In Blue's backyard is **an apple** tree.
Blue picks some **apples**—one, two, three.
"***Allo! Allo!***" Mrs. Pepper cries.
"I'll put those in my **apple** pies!"

Baby Bear calls, "Blue, come and look
At the pictures in my big *B* book.
There are birds, a boat, and bubbles, too."
"I see a bumblebee!" says Blue.

Cc

Cookies, **chocolates**, and yummy **cupcakes**
Are some of the goodies Mr. Salt makes.
Blue **colors** with **crayons** in a **coloring** book.
Then she sips hot **cocoa** in the Breakfast Nook.

Dd

Shovel likes to dig sand way down deep.
Pail piles it up in a great big heap.
They make a dragon, a deer, and a duck,
Then dump the rest in a red dump truck.

Ee

Mr. Salt puts eggs in things he likes to bake.
He's using eight eggs in this birthday cake.
He has the eggs ready. Can you see
What else he needs for his recipe?

The Felt Friends like to play a game
And flip and flop inside their frame.
Fred and Fran make circles and a square.
What other shapes can you find there?

Gg

Magenta loves her glasses. They help her see.
She gazes at a goose and a bright green *G*.
A ghost starts to giggle and then says, "Boo!"
Magenta says, "Green Puppy, I know it's you!"

Blue skidoos to a farm. A **horse** and **hen**
Tell **her**, "We're **happy** to see you again."
Blue wears a **hat** and **helps** rake with a **hoe**
Then **hops** in the **hay** before it's time to go.

Ii

Icy cold **ice** cream **is** sweet to eat.
It's Blue's and Periwinkle's favorite treat.
In an **ice**-cream cone or **in** a cup,
The two friends love to eat **it** up!

Jj

Blue likes to jam on her jelly-jar drums.
She plays jazzy rhythms while Magenta hums.
Periwinkle comes along and joins his friends.
They all jump for joy until the music ends.

Orange Kitten and Blue fly a king-size kite.
The key is to keep the string good and tight.
Magenta kicks a ball to Purple Kangaroo
And plays him a song on her new kazoo.

Ll

Blue gets **letters** whether it's rainy or sunny.
They're delivered by Mailbox, who's very funny.
He makes her **laugh** and often sings
When **leaving** all the mail he brings.

Miss Marigold teaches **Magenta** and Blue.
They love **Miss Marigold** and learning, too.
Will it be **math**, **music**, or **maps** today?
"**Maybe** all three," **Magenta** and Blue say.

Nn

Blue and Green Puppy take a nature hike.
They walk through the forest wherever they like.
They meet a little squirrel with a nut in a tree
And nine birds in a nest singing happily.

Oo

Slippery Soap often has an odd notion—
He imagines his bathtub is really the ocean!
He plays with his octopus, rows with his oars,
And dreams of adventures on faraway shores.

Pp

Periwinkle writes to his **pen pal**, **Plum**.
"I have **plenty** of friends and hope you'll come
To visit me here again someday.
I can't wait to see you—**please** come to **play**!"

Qq

Blue loves to ask **questions** so she can find out
What the world around her is all about.
She **quietly** thinks in the Thinking Chair
And comes up with answers while sitting there.

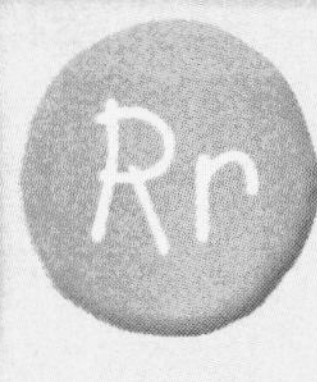

The **rain** comes down in drips and drops.
It **rains** and **rains** and never stops.
But Blue and Green Puppy don't complain.
They wear **red rubber** boots in the **rain**.

Ss

Sidetable Drawer really loves to **sing**.
She sings songs about everything.
The Handy Dandy Notebook can be found
Snug in **Sidetable** Drawer, all **safe** and **sound**.

Tt

Tickety Tock rings her bells and **then**
Helps Blue practice counting one **to ten**.
When **they** get **to ten**, it’s **time** for bed.
Blue sleeps as numbers **twirl** in her head.

Uu

Periwinkle says, “Let’s tidy up, Blue!”
Underneath the washer, he finds a shoe.
Blue finds an umbrella and says, “I know!
This is where the umbrellas go!”

Blue loves giving presents on Valentine's Day.
She can't wait to give her valentines away.
She gives them to friends and never forgets
Mrs. Pepper's vase of pretty violets.

Blue loves winter when the thick wet snow
Swirls around her while the cold winds blow.
She thinks it's pretty, so soft and white,
And perfect for a snowball fight!

X is a letter Blue likes a lot.
Can you see where X marks the spot?
If you look closely, you will see
Four letter X's easily!

Yy

"**Yippee!**" **Yellow** Kitten says to Blue.
"I have a **yellow yo-yo** to share with **you**!
Let's eat **yummy yogurt**, then go out to play.
I'll show **you** the trick I learned **yesterday**!"

Zz
"Zowie," says Blue. "We made it to *Z!*
We zipped and zoomed past *A, B,* and *C!*
There isn't one letter that we had to skip.
How many are left? Zero! Zilch! Zip!"

O
H
A
L
D
R
T
E
X
Y
G
J
N
W
M
B

Can you find all the letters one last time?
Thanks for helping—that's the end of our rhyme!